Sage'

Now stop the music,
Quiet down.
Pause and listen
To the sounds...

Tweet Tweet... Tweet Tweet!
Large and small
Birds passing through.

Woof Woof! Woof Woof!

Is that a dog barking at you?

Bzzzz Bzzzz! Bzzzz Bzzzz!
Busy bees zip and fly.

Hummm, Hummm...
Hummm, Hummm...
A gentle breeze blows on by.

Sage listens closely
To the world all around,
And decides to make music
With all of nature's sounds.

With a **1**, a **2**, and a **1**, **2**, **3**...

Sage dances and grooves
To the rhythm of nature's beat!

And in the quiet
When the music is done
Sage falls fast asleep
To the gentle Hummm Hummm...

Awake or asleep
Sage is aware
That when you listen closely...
Music is EVERYWHERE!

The PUMPKINHEADS ANSWER:

What is your favorite instrument?

Ella: Violin ♥

Lulu: Guitar!